Dear Parents:

Children learn to read in stages, and all children develop reading skills at different ages. **Ready Readers**™ were created to promote children's interest in reading and to increase their reading skills. **Ready Readers**™ are written on two levels to accommodate children ranging in age from three through eight. These stages are meant to be used only as a guide.

Stage 1: Preschool-Grade 1
Stage 1 books are written in very short, simple sentences with large type. They are perfect for children who are getting ready to read or are just becoming familiar with reading on their own.

Stage 2: Grades 1-3
Stage 2 books have longer sentences and are a bit more complex. They are suitable for children who are able to read but still may need help.

All the **Ready Readers**™ tell varied, easy-to-follow stories and are colorfully illustrated. Reading will be fun, and soon your child will not only be ready, but eager to read.

SLOW TURTLE
SAVES THE DAY

Written by Agatha Brown
Illustrated by Jo-Ellen Bosson

Modern Publishing
A Division of Unisystems, Inc.
New York, New York 10022

This is Slow Turtle. He takes his time everywhere he goes. He often stops to smell the flowers.

Slow Turtle has many friends.
One of his friends is...

...Gentle Lamb. She likes to chase butterflies.

Gentle Lamb has many friends. One of her friends is...

...Hungry Bear. He likes to eat and eat and eat.

Hungry Bear has many friends
too. One friend is...

...Proud Peacock.

He likes to show off his beautiful feathers.

Slow Turtle, Gentle Lamb, Hungry Bear and Proud Peacock are all good friends. Sometimes they play together.

One day, Proud Peacock got his tail stuck in a bush. Everyone helped to get him out. The friends always help each other.

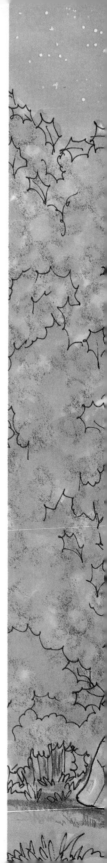

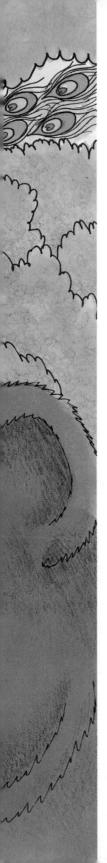

Hungry Bear must eat
and eat and eat to get ready
for his long winter's sleep,
so, his friends bring him
food.

On Sunday at noon the four friends plan to give another friend, Busy Beaver, a medal. They want to honor him for building his dam all by himself.

But Hungry Bear did not think that Slow Turtle would make it to the big meadow on time.

"I hope that you can move faster or you will miss the whole thing," Hungry Bear said to Slow Turtle.

Slow Turtle was sad. He wanted to be there for Busy Beaver.

The next day, Slow Turtle
worked out.

He crawled to the left.

He crawled to the right.

He crawled to the left and right
as fast as he could.

On Sunday, Hungry
Bear took off for the Big
Meadow. He had his bat so
that he could play ball
on the way. He also had
Beaver's medal.

"I hope that you make
it," he said to Slow Turtle.

"I will! I will!" Slow
Turtle said.

But Slow Turtle could not help himself.

He stopped to smell the flowers.

He stopped to say hello to a busy ant.

He stopped to look at a mushroom.

That's when he found a round and shiny medal hanging on a blue ribbon.

Slow Turtle put the medal around his neck. Then he went left and right and left again as fast as he could to the Big Meadow.

When Slow Turtle got to the Big Meadow, his friends were looking everywhere for the lost medal.

"Hooray!" they shouted when they saw Slow Turtle, "You found Busy Beaver's medal!"

"I was running so fast that I didn't know I lost it," Hungry Bear said.

"Sometimes it is good to take your time," Slow Turtle said.

"You are so right," Hungry Bear said, "You saved the day Slow Turtle!"

Slow Turtle was proud!